Brian Douglas Beverly

HOBO II
THE JOURNEY

Order this book online at www.trafford.com
or email orders@trafford.com

Most Trafford titles are also available at major online book retailers.

Print information available on the last page.

ISBN: 978-1-4251-2345-1 (sc)

Trafford rev. 07/20/2022

 www.trafford.com

North America & international
toll-free: 844-688-6899 (USA & Canada)
fax: 812 355 4082

This: The continuation of Clarence Taylor, has him well on his way to Toledo, Ohio and very much in life— a hobo. He will get a new name and work with migrant workers, and travel as itinerants do.

HOBO II

THE JOURNEY

Prologue

From out of the wooded forest, and alongside of the cottonfield comes a train. That's held fast to the iron rails. It's coming from a farmer's town that's not heavily populated and no longer can manage. Because it is the years of the Great Depression, that happened after the Great Stock Market crash. Clarence Taylor, who stole aboard in one of the boxcars, is lying down on the wooden floor—vibrant from the rumbling of the train. He sits up and gets his bundle, where there are some biscuits and apples he took from his mother's kitchen before he left. A lot of the paranoia is gone out of him because it is all so very real. The day is not so very cold, nor does it have the harsh winds blowing as it can be here in the winter's month of February 1932. After eating two of the biscuits, and one apple, Clarence lies back down.

Prologue

The engineer is at the helm and he can see off a far, a great distance into the countryside. And there is the breakman and the fireman. The fireman is shoveling coal into the furnace and has it moving out fast. The conductor and flagman are seated in the caboose. They're sitting high up in seats to keep on the lookout. And it's been nearly another one hundred miles that it will be taking on water once again at a water trough.

Clarence realizes he is well on his way and deep into the train's movements. And now he's falling asleep as he lies there.

Cotton field

Roundhouse

1

Several hours pass by very quickly for Clarence Taylor. And what he doesn't know is the railroad crew got a message at the depot in Virginia before leaving, to head south — go to Florida. So they switched tracks, and they're coming into a roundhouse in South Carolina that's along the way. And it is night now.

"Hey, you get out of the way!"

"What? Who said that?" Clarence jumps down to the ground from the boxcar as he hears a voice from underneath calling up to him.

"I said get out of the way, so I can climb out!" Clarence bends over to see who it is, and there's a hobo lying on a board, which he placed on a rod that's to the suspension. Clarence straightens up and moves back and the hobo climbs out from underneath. Hurriedly, he sprints over to where Clarence is standing, telling him to move out—get going.

"Come on, let's get moving. We'll get behind those trees over there before the shacks see us. So we won't have to pay bo money."

They run into the woods and stand side by side behind a very big tree, talking just above a whisper.

"That looks scary riding underneath there, where you was at," says Clarence.

"Oh, don't you know? I'm a trapeze artist. I can do it."

"A trapeze artist?"

"Yeah, that's right. I'm rails trapeze Maxwell."

"What is that?"

"That's what I'm known for ridin'. I carved a groove down the middle of a wooden plank, and set it down on top of the rod there, that's to the suspension, in the undercarriage. And as it swings, I swing my ticket. Now that's the trapeze artist hopping trains."

"I see. But what did you mean pay bo money?"

"Now that's some more you don't know. I saw how you climbed aboard. And I could see you ain't been hoboin'."

"No, I ain't been. That's the only time I ever hopped a train. But I talked to someone who did. Me and him was fishing. And he told me something about it before he got shot thievin'. My town has gotten to be pretty bad off. There's no jobs or anything much to speak on. So I just took to it," explains Clarence.

"Yeah...you bet ya. And its gonna be bad now too! Besides, what I mean bo money is what money you have now that you hoppin' trains—a hobo. And the shacks are the railroad crew."

"I know what the shacks are, I used to work for the railroad."

"Well, then, you must understand too, if the shacks see that ya stole aboard, they'll shake you down for it," finishes the hobo, Rails Trapeze Maxwell. They become silent, still behind the trees looking out at the train, as it's getting filled with water. And it is lubricated as they wipe the grime off the boiler. Also here in a roundhouse a train can get stored and have light maintenance performed on it. But this one will keep on its way.

The Jacksonville train station

2

Morning comes with the train pulling into the Jacksonville train yard. Clarence jumps from the boxcar and Rails Trapeze Maxwell escapes from underneath. They manage to get where some people are near the depot. Communicating with them is not too difficult because people are sociable there. Rails Trapeze leaves Clarence and disappears in the crowd. And it's a very large train station, with all of the options. Some workers working the freight line are busying themselves very diligently. The farmers come through with lots of vegetables from out of their gardens.

"Hello, sir. I see it's busy around here. I'm looking to get some work. How can I work the freight line?" Clarence asks a man who's standing there.

"Yeah...sure...and I'll bet you're another one that's not from around here."

"Um...no, I'm not from around here."

"Are you a migrant worker, because most everybody is?"

"Just looking to get that much ahead, that's all."

"Well, it's all spoken for. But there's a train leaving tomorrow morning headed for Naples. I'll be gettin' aboard that one to go pick oranges. If you want to, you can come along. But you better go get your name put on the list."

"Naples, where is that?"

"It's south of here and on the West side. Where the Gulf is."

"Here in Florida you mean?"

"Yes here in Florida. That'll be in the morning in front of the depot. And that's where you go sign up now. You're just in time for that. By the way, have you got a name?"

"Yes its Clarence, and you? What's your name?"

"My name is Alfred."

Clarence goes to put his name on the list for picking oranges in Naples, and looks for somewhere to go until then. He is very hungry at this time and decides to go for something to eat. He walks away from the train station and walks more into the city of Jacksonville, Florida. The stock market crash has taken a toll on the economy here as well as in Virginia.

Clarence walks a good distance away and stops on a street corner, looking in all directions, he doesn't see any place to get something to eat. So he continues on his way and finds a bread line to get into down left from the next corner. The long line of people keep moving, so that it isn't too terribly long of a wait before Clarence reaches the loaf of bread and gets a cup of warm tea. Intermixing with the others is not too difficult, so he is at ease with himself.

"Hello, I'm Clarence," he tells a man who's standing there, with his bread and cup of tea too.

"Hello Clarence—Clarence who?"

"Clarence Taylor, I'm from Virginia. I can see its all right around here."

"Oh, you come in from Virginia. Almost everyone's from some place else these days."

"I'll be pick 'n oranges in Naples in the mornin'."

"I just bet ya are. I'll be pickin' vegetables for a farmer next week. And it'll be well worth the wait, too! Because he's a farmer that grows one of the largest gardens, and is hard ta get with. He pays in cash too, and nothin' other. It could be that we go before. So I'm sure to keep myself visible. Whether it's across the street he said or up on the corner. That he may pick me up in his truck up there."

"Hey that sounds like you got a good idea," says Clarence.

"Yes I do have."

"What's your name? ask Clarence.

"Its Bernard Lancer. But they call me Bernie."

"Ok, Its Bernie. Do you know where I can bed down for the night? Somewhere close by here I mean?" asks Clarence.

"Sure, there's two places. One's over on the next street,

and the other is a little peace from here, but you can walk it," says Bernie.

Clarence gets the details on just where the boarding houses are, and finishes eating his bread and drinks the last drop from his teacup. Then he walks to the one that's over on the next street. And within a few minutes, he is standing in front of a big red brick house that has a black iron gate and fence all the way around it. He opens the gate and steps in on the pavement, that leads up to the giant porch, where there's two big front doors together. Clarence is knocking on the doors, and it takes very little time for an elderly man to answer.

"Yes, who is it that's calling?" the man asks with only one door open and his head sticking out.

"I'm Clarence Taylor, sir. Someone told me there might be rooms here, and I might bed down for the night."

"Well you could, if there were any available, but there is none."

"I'll be moving along then," Clarence walks a half-mile more, and gets to the other boarding house. It's made of wood, and painted white. The big two-story boarding house stretches across the lawn through the backyard. Clarence is upon the porch knocking, but this time there's only one door. And it's in the afternoon by now. A very tall woman age forty opens the door.

"Hi there, would you like a room?" she asks.

"Yeah, if you got one available," answers Clarence.

"That I do, and you can come in." Clarence steps in

and follows her past the staircase and into the front room, where there's a very big roll top desk. She sits down at it and tells Clarence to pull up a chair as well.

"I'm Gail Winston, what is your name?"

"I'm Clarence Taylor."

"I've got just what you're looking for upstairs," she says smiling nice and coming onto Clarence.

"Do you want the room for only one night or will you be staying longer?" she continues.

"Its just for tonight, then I'll be headed back to the train station so I can catch a train bound for Naples in the morning, to go pick oranges with migrant workers."

"I see...of course, you've got to work the best you can get it."

"That's right, I signed up for it this morning."

"Maybe you can come back here after you do that."

"Yeah, sure."

"If not for a room, maybe to say hello again."

"You know I'm glad you brought that up, because I feel there's some chemistry between the two of us too," says Clarence.

Gail finds Clarence to be an attractive man. She keeps smiling and coming onto him. She has big bold brown eyes, dark black hair that has some gray. And is a very tall shapely woman who also is brown-skinned like Clarence.

"Yes, the chemistry is right," says Gail.

"So you're not married?" Clarence asks.

The Journey

"No I'm not, as well as you I'm sure."

"No but I was gonna get married, until she died here recently." "Oh, she died?" "That's right, she died of pneumonia just this winter's passing. Before I hopped a train, and winded up down here in Florida."

"And you hopped a train? I'm sorry to hear some one is dead on your behalf, but I must tell you that you'll be just another hobo if you don't make your mind up as to where you'll be staying put."

They talk just a few minutes more, and touch base with each other's feelings. She takes the money he needs to pay, and then escorts him to his room. "You must want something to eat at this time," says Gail Winston.

"I got in a bread line this morning before coming here, and that's it. So if you can spare it, I'll take something more."

"Yes, I do have some soup for my tenants. You can get a bowl a day as long as you're here paying. They're big bowls, too. I'll go get it for you." She steps out closing the door behind her, and walks through the hallway, then down the stair steps to the kitchen.

Clarence puts his bundle on the bed and opens it. He takes from it a fresh change of clothes. Then goes over to the other side of the room where there's a wash basin and washes up before changing his clothes. He thinks of home and what his mother's reaction must have been to his leaving. Clarence is changed into his other clothes and settles in for the evenings coming. He puts his bundle down on the floor near the dresser and then sits in a chair. Gail is knocking softly at the door. She is back with a dinner tray that has a big bowl of chicken noodle soup placed on it, and two slices of buttered toast. She also manages a glass of ice-tea.

Clarence stands up from the chair and opens the door to find her there.

"Good you brought me some soup."

"Yes and I had to take time to warm it up. I'll put it down on the table, there next to your chair. He closes the door and rushes over to where she is, then immediately goes for the dinner tray and attacks his bowl of soup.

"My goodness, you must be starving."

"The bread was only so much earlier."

"My big bowl of chicken noodle soup will fill you up. And there is toast with it too, that you can see."

"Thank you for all of this. The other tenants must be crazy for you as I am."

"Of course, but here with you more so it's the chemistry, like you said before. Now quit talking with your mouth full." Gail places herself on the side of the bed and talks of them spending time together. She is very pretty sitting there in her dress, with great sex appeal. She raises her dress up above her knees. Then strokes her legs with one hand at the calf, down to her ankles.

"I'll bet you'd like to come here after you finish eating Clarence?" she says passionately. By now he has eaten half the big bowl of soup.

The Journey

"Well, the rest of this can keep till later on," says Clarence. "That's right, so come here." Gail reaches the blanket at the pillows and pulls it away, exposing the sheets underneath. Without saying another word, Clarence gets up from the table and goes over to where she is.

Still sitting, Gail puckers her lips for Clarence to give her a kiss. Clarence comes for it as though a magnet attracted to steel. Their lovemaking is with much ecstasy, that they are so physically attractive to each other. And the height of their stimulation causes them to collapse in each other's arms.

Now they've fallen asleep on into the night.

3

And at this same time in the small Virginian town where Clarence Taylor comes from, his mother Sally is soothing her husband, Nathaniel Williams, who is called Nate.

She brings a pail of hot water from off the top of the hot burning coal stove and pours it into Nate's bath. He is soaking in the tub more than half full of water. The coal stove burning hot, also has the house heated to protect it from the cold outdoors.

Whereas in Florida, the climate is much warmer. After Sally pours the hot water into the tub, she goes into the living room and looks out of the window at the outdoors. Night comes quickly during the winter months. She can only see the bare trees and that there 's hardly any stars visible in the sky up above.

The Journey

    Nate has been out working today. He manages to get work chopping firewood. He and the other men stack the firewood on in the same location where the coal is kept. The townspeople can purchase it for a price. Its been the holidays since after Clarence's girlfriend, Norma's death. And this year in its beginning is not anymore promising than the year before.

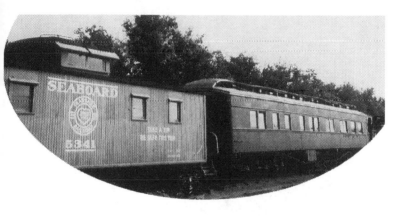

The train that has Clarence and Alfred on board, going to Naples.

4

In the morning, Clarence is quickly dressed and goes down the stairs for the front door of the boarding house.

"Clarence wait!" shouts Gail Winston.

He stops and turns to her, and sees her sitting at the desk. He goes over to where she is.

"What," he asks.

"You're going in such a hurry, let's talk about last night."

"I need to be at the train station this morning before long. I told you about it."

"Yes I know that. But last night is some business, too. I'd like you to leave two dollars on the desk before you go."

"I thought we were together, because we like it."

"That's right, we liked it. But still a lady's got ta do

whatever she can to make ends meet. So pay the money. And just you know I like ya, and come back."

Clarence gets his purse and unsnaps it, then reaches in and brings the two dollars out she requested. He puts the money down on the desk. Then he walks to the train station. He is lined up with all of the other workers for role call. They walk past a desk, with someone seated there to check their names off, instead of calling their names out to them. Clarence sees Alfred standing in line and is calling out to him. "Say Alfred, I see you made it in this morning too. Well, good."

"Yeah, that's right. Standing in line gettin' your name checked off is the thing ta do now. Then it'll be all aboard," says Alfred.

After roll call is done they have time to stand around and talk some more. Alfred had gone to pick fruit as a migrant worker before, as well he's from Jacksonville, Florida. He's telling Clarence about it so he can make good when the time comes. The railroad tracks at the train station are many, and all laid out evenly in rows. Yet it's as though they're scattered about. The train going on its way gets on a long straight and narrow iron path that's headed out of town. Clarence is sitting in the window seat and he can see the outdoors plant life, and it's not like Virginia, the trees are palm trees.

"We'll be there just before noon, and then they'll be driving us to the orange grove in trucks," says Alfred.

"Yeah, the week will do me some good for the money. And then I got ta be gettin' on my way. I'm gonna go to

Toledo, Ohio to work in a factory," says Clarence.

"Oh...so you don't say," replied Alfred.

"That's right, I was headed there on a train from Virginia. It switch tracks and came here instead. Once this is done I'm gettin' on my way," finishes Clarence.

"Yeah I hear ya. But as it stands right now, you best look forward to living in a tent. Because when we get to it they're gonna give you a bed roll and your sleeping quarters is gonna be in a tent camped out with a bunch of migrant workers pick 'n oranges. And that's what everybody's gonna get to be, is plain ole migrant worker," says Alfred."

Clarence says nothing after that. He is looking out of the window at the country sites in thought. A very large man with a white brim on his head, who's name is Mister Quarterman, is standing outside on the front lawn of his house. He is eating an apple and using his pocket knife to cut slices from it and eat bites as he talks to his wife, who's sitting on the front porch swing.

"I'd imagine it's gonna be some more colored people when the train gets in from Jacksonville today," he says.

"Yeah... maybe, there's a lot of them out at the orange grove now. That and the Spanish people," she replies.

"I know there is, the colored people speak English though. Whereas I have trouble communicating with the Spanish people."

"What are you doing with that apple? How's come you don't pore yourself another cup of coffee?"

The Journey

"Because I got it all this morning. I done had all of the coffee I'm gonna get. I walk out here with this apple because I feel to have the rest of my morning this way."

"Ok, you go ahead, and I won't say no more."

He is looking forward to this afternoon's coming of the train, that has the migrant workers on board. Because he'll be able to get a lot of oranges picked and impress the buyers at the scales.

5

Haddy, Jane, and Mary, are seated in Joe and Betty's kitchen-in here in their small Virginian town, in Tidewater Virginia. They're eating breakfast. Haddy and Mary have pancakes with maple syrup, and Jane has two biscuits with honey. Also all of them have spread butter.

"I talked to Sally yesterday, and she said Clarence left," says Jane.

"Oh he did?" replies Haddy.

"Yes, and she's still waiting to hear from him," Jane again.

"Did he go by himself?" asks Mary.

"Clarence talked of leaving on a train, and didn't say anything about anyone else. Sally guessed that's what he did, on his own," Jane explains.

The Journey

Martha Johnson is waiting tables at the kitchen-in. Her mother used to work there as well. But Joe and Betty had cut back on expenses, so they let her go. She asks if Martha could work in her place for a lot less money and Martha can get by.

"Well hello Martha, I see they got you busy around here today. And that's good," replies Jane. "Yes, that's right, and I'll be workin' everyday this week. Its going good around here because they've got the prices fixed for the way money is these days," says Martha.

"Yeah, that's good. But we should let you get back to work, so you can stay with it," says Haddy. Mary says nothing, but she is looking up at Martha with eyes wide open and smiling, in acknowledgment. All of the tables are filled up with people in the kitchen-in. Some of them gesture to refill their coffee cup or come with hot water for tea.

Naples Depot

Orange Grove

6

The train has just arrived at the Atlantic coastline depot, in Naples Florida. And Clarence Taylor wants to find a nearby telephone to call his neighbor Gretchen, who lives across the street from his mother's house in Virginia. To let them know he is all right and to tell his whereabouts. But they're told to keep together, and line up alongside of the depot, to keep accounted for as they disembark the train. He is thinking of getting to the telegraph operator, and sending a message that way. Since they have to stay together in the respect that they do.

"That's it! That's right! You people get lined up close to me here as you get off the train," commands the foreman. "And if there's any stragglers they best get over here where everybody's gettin' at too. You get abreast, so we can take another head count," he continues. "And be sure everyone that's on the roster got aboard in Jacksonville, and didn't fizzle back and not make it. Next we're gonna load ya up on them trucks over there, and get you all out at the orange grove where it's all at," finishes the foreman.

The superintendent is driving up the road in his pick-up truck. He can see just ahead all that's been aboard.

"That there comin' is Mr. Quarterman, the superintendent," says the foreman who's taking the head count. He parks it in the dirt, steps out and is walking towards all of the abreast.

"Well now, you all should do quite nicely out at the orange grove. You all look mighty fine to me," says Mr. Quarterman approaching.

"Thank you sir," says the foreman on behalf of all the men. It wasn't long after that, they loaded the trucks up with themselves and headed for the orange grove. The trucks can go only so fast, driving on the rocky dirt roads that are full of potholes.

The slow ride and its whereabouts, has it to Clarence Taylor—more journey. The trucks come driving into camp that evening and tents have been pitched for their living quarters. There is a place to take a bath in a big tin-tub, or down in a big wooden barrel. And the cooking is done outside over an open fire.

"I got ta have you all line up again at that tent over there, and get your issue," says the foreman.

"Here you are fella, next one in line," says one of the migrant workers who's assigned to keeping up with the supplies.

"After he gives it to ya— next you go see Henry over there, and he'll get cha put to a tent," the foreman again.

Once Clarence gets his bed roll, he walks over to where Henry is standing and is assigned to a tent. Then Clarence goes inside and unrolls the blanket on top of a cot. And lays himself down. He is lying there on his back, looking upward at the ceiling of the tent, in thought, just as he did in his bedroom in Tidewater, Virginia. He is thinking of his people back home, as far as what they must have going on since he's been gone away. Mr. Quarterman is in one of the cabins there in the orange grove. And he is talking to some of the other men about the up coming election for the president.

"This here Franklin Delano Roosevelt is making a lot of noise—calling it the forgotten man. He's saying something about a new deal. It seems things are gonna go his way in this here election."

Its 1932 and Franklin Delano Roosevelt is campaigning for president of the United States of America. He promises to get fast relief to the country by starting some relief programs. And he promises to get the country's economy back. And look into the future to keep from having a depression again.

"Yeah, but it's gonna be hard for him ta go against President Hoover, who's it already," says one of the men who's there at the cabin too.

"No… this here Roosevelt puts it where president Herbert Clark Hoover didn't. Hoover said it was gonna turn the corner and talked out of all that optimism that he did. And things still ain't right yet. Roosevelt ta champagne, is saying ta have something come from the government for it. Whereas Hoover believes not to. That's enough talk tonight, for what comes in the mornings around here. That cha know what your gonna have picking oranges. I'll see ya then," finishes the superintendent Mr. Quarterman.

Alfred manages to get in the same tent as Clarence.

"Well hello there Clarence, I see you got comfortable," says Alfred.

"Yeah I wanted to get laid down after it's been the trip down here. I didn't know it be this far," says Clarence.

"Oh yeah...that's right. I may owe you an apology for not saying how far. It's just that I've been at this here and didn't think ta tell ya how far."

"That's all right, because I didn't know what I was gonna do anyways. Since the train brought me here to Florida instead of taking me to Ohio."

"Oh yeah, Ohio. You were saying something about that."

"I want to go and see if I can work in a factory in Toledo."

"Well... now you might get a train out of here headed to Tampa that'll take ya."

"That's what I was thinkin.' And that train station here in Naples impresses me too."

Clarence and Alfred talked a bit more about what it is to get any Atlantic Coast Line train out of Naples bound for Tampa, to get North to Ohio.

And it just so happens that they got to the orange grove in time for the final meal of the day. It's a big pot of beef stew cooking over an open fire. Clarence and Alfred go outside their tent and stand in line with the others. They've been given a tin pan, a wooden spoon, and a tin-cup.

People are trying to decide which way to vote. Champagnes for the presidency are under way here in 1932. And it's well known by now that the country is bad off with its money schemes. So the most careful business management is sought after. Patriotism throughout the land is as though it's displayed on one big billboard. A traditional hard working family provider, is said for the American man. And the spreading of the news behooves the matters to the individual.

7

Here on the outer banks in Atlanta, Georgia, there's a hobo jungle. Those people are very much alive—moving about and scrounging up whatever food they can find. They're grouped in one big bunch, and it's as though they've made their own broken-down village. It's foul in the air as it is in a land field where garbage gets dumped. They've got old messed-up shoes on their feet, and their clothes are made of rags. Hobo jungles though, usually are formed-up in a place where there's running water. They wash their clothes in big pots of boiling water and are sure to do so for the times when they go into town. He or she'll get penalized by the police for vagrancy if they are seen too dirty.

A very large black man is sitting on the ground here in the hobo jungle. And he is taking care of his oldest and

Brian Douglas Beverly

greatest friend. His friend is dying because of tuberculosis. He is a very thin white man, as though bed-ridden there in the black man's arms. The both of them are middle aged, fifty. There's enough rice and beans scrounged up to feed. But the man with tuberculosis can't eat and coughs too much.

"Aren't ya gonna eat your plate up?"

"Not yet, my appetites no good and I'm having one of my coughing spells."

The night is no longer young, and it's a full moon, that the moon's glow is all over the place.

"Hey I never told ya. I love ya," says the white man.

8

At first Clarence has to get used to being high up on a ladder, and reach out as far as he can to pick the ripest oranges. Once he's filled a bag hanging from around his neck, he then climbs down the ladder and dumps them into a tub. And there are some who come to dump the tubs into the back of the trucks after they're filled up with oranges. Clarence slept all through the night, because of the restless train ride yesterday. This morning had come very quickly. And the day is going by just as swiftly that it is already in the afternoon.

"Come on and lets go on break, people! The boss man said ta knock off for a while," shouts one of the migrant workers. And everyone picking oranges climb down from their ladder and dump off into the tub whatever in the amounts they have in their bag. Then everyone goes over to where lunch is staged. And the foreman is nearby with the superintendent. There's ham sandwiches, and vegetables from a garden. And there's some fresh squeezed-orange juice, as well as a large barrel full of drinking water.

"How do you like gettin' that orange juice along with everything else, that it's out here as it is?" asks the superintendent.

For Clarence it's an unexpected welcoming, that he has been without fresh squeezed-orange juice since after Mr. Foster had to let him go at the depot.

He finds a place to sit in the grass along with some others.

"You watch sittin' on the ground, Clarence. Because there's fire ants down here in Florida. They'll overtake ya and eat you alive. If any of them around ya get ta slappin' down on himself, you get up fast and move away," shouts Alfred at Clarence from the back of a pick-up truck where he and a bunch of other men are sitting and eating their sandwiches.

Clarence takes note to what Alfred said, but he stays seated on the ground. Before long ants come about and chase them away. After lunch, they all are back to work with good clear vision picking the oranges. As though revived from a hallucinated state of being.

Clarence is fast up and down the ladder now, and quick to reposition it. There's very little talking, a lot of the sounds is the rattling from the trees. And the sound of the oranges getting picked is like the snapping off of a small brittle twig.

Now the sun is going down, and makes the haze in the day. They're all back at the tents and getting the final meal of the day, and it's the same as before.

"Some more of that beef stew's gonna go down good about now, says Clarence.

"That's hobo stew out here on the beat 'n path," says Alfred.

"Yeah...well it's doing alright for the time I'll be here," says Clarence.

"I hope you're not going after only one week," says Alfred.

"Yep, that's it. Then I'm gonna go."

"I'll tell ya now, we're gonna be at this here for another one and something. With just this much people working. And it just might be worth your while to stick around."

"No, I'll be gettin' on my way. I heard 'em talkin' about another train that's comin' and I'm gonna be gettin' on it. They were saying it's headed to Tampa and switch off to something that'll be going north, just where I'm headed."

"Ok, but don't you forget to say good bye before you go."

They have their tin plates heaped over with hobo stew and sit down on half broken-up old wooden chairs placed outside in front of their tent. A tall lanky man with two others is walking past Clarence and Alfred, and he doesn't like Clarence.

"There you are sit 'n their eatin' your stew." The man-walking pass says to Clarence.

"I notice you out at the orange grove and around here some. And something's to ya. That I don't like you," he finishes.

"Well now that's news to me boy," says Clarence.

"That's right I never told ya until now."

"What's gonna be to it?" asks Clarence as he puts his plate down and is standing erect at the sarcastic man to face him down. Alfred still sitting, eying the both of them speaks up.

"It seems ta me like the two of you are even ta fight. But ya shouldn't do it now, because it's been a hot and hard working day. That ya need ta eat and bed down."

"Maybe he's right, then it'll keep till mornin'."

He walks away hard staring at Clarence after he speaks his final words. Clarence looks down at Alfred and nods his head saying "That'll be just fine" and then picks his plate up off the ground and sits back down.

And the morning comes bright and sun shiny. Fast coming about like the flip of a switch. "Hey you in there! Get outside!"

"What ya got it in for him for?" asks a man, the both of them just on the outside of Clarence and Alfred's tent.

"I said I don't like 'em. That's why!"

Alfred comes out first fixing his suspenders up over his shoulders to hold up his trousers.

"I mean that other fella, where's he?"

"Clarence you best get out here for what's doin'," shouts Alfred.

The Journey

Clarence comes outside fully dressed to confront the matter. "You still want 'n me boy?" asks Clarence without any fright of the event that's taking place about him.

"Yeah I mean you, now lets have at it!"

At that moment Clarence is to his front, the both of them with dukes up. He throws the first punch at Clarence. It's a long droopy swinging right fist that comes for Clarence's jaw. And he ducks his head and the flying fist misses. Then comes another after Clarence, just as he straightens up. But this time it's a left fist across. Clarence throws his head back and gets out of the way of it. Immediately Clarence charges back into the tall lanky man, and punches him in the belly. And he sounds a loud grunt. Before he can straighten up Clarence hits him again with an upper cut to the face, causing him to fall backwards to the ground. A crowd forms shouting for more fighting.

"Hey you, get up! Is that all ya got?" shouts a man in the crowd.

"Yeah you started it! Come again!" Shouts another from the crowd.

"He aint gettin' up."

"Y...He's knocked out."

"Lets bring 'em to."

"Yeah...but cha know what? This one here wins the fist fight."

"All right break it up! Lets break it up!" Commands the foreman as he's making his way through the crowd. He just got there with the trucks.

"Now you men break this up and hurry and get your breakfast. We're all suppose to be working before long," the foreman again.

"Yeah Clarence, you done enough, so let's go," says Alfred.

"Wait a minute, I'm gonna talk to 'em and see what he had it in for me for."

"Ok, but you heard the foreman."

"Yeah I heard 'em."

The man is up on his feet. Clarence and Alfred walk over to where he is standing. "Hey you! What did you have it in for me for?" asks Clarence.

"Forget it, it was nothing."

"No, it was something, alright. Just what was it that had you after me?"

"Let's just say I don't like you, because your not like I am. As we all are. Your different."

"That's right, I got grown up. And I can see you been scrounging up what you can all of your time."

"Like I said, forget it."

The feeling Clarence has from his new surroundings is as though he dropped out of society as far as who he really is. And the will he has to reach Ohio is overwhelming. But he tries not to show his emotions. Clarence is becoming homesick and wants to get the feelings of being home somehow.

The Journey

The week is ended and Clarence gets his pay of five dollars along with the others. He has gone back to the depot, where he is about to get aboard a passenger train bound for Tampa. But before he does, he calls his neighbor from across the street.

"Hi, its me Clarence, I want to talk to mom and tell her where I am and what's going on with me."

"They've gone out for the day, no ones home," says Gretchen.

Clarence leaves her a detailed message about himself. And says he'll try and call again.

The train in Naples gets all aboard on time as expected. But the passenger train from out of Tampa, that'll be going through Georgia, and Tennessee for Kentucky and then Ohio, is scheduled to be in Tampa tomorrow. However, the train Clarence is aboard will get there tonight. So he is going to spend the night at the depot, there in Tampa, instead of going to a boarding house as he did in Jacksonville.

This time the train ride for Clarence is pleasant and not the intensity it was before. He gets sacked out in his chair, and is taking a nap. He had to finish the day working at the orange grove, and then he got his pay.

Tampa Union Train Station

The inside of Tampa Union Train Station where you purchase tickets

9

There are people who have always worked hard and kept long hours. But now most of them are at the soup kitchen, and standing in bread lines, for the charity of all that. Families are put to poverty, and cast out, because they can no longer pay rent and mortgage. Their automobile got repossessed as well. And if there's any money loaned out among friends or family members, it could not be repaid. Kids are barely clothed and sometimes become ill from their living condition.

As time progresses, families that are poverty stricken take shelter in a lot of the lower cost houses available. And more then one family lives together in some of the low cost houses or run-down old tenant buildings, that are nearly condemned. The charity of all this is hardly provided for single people, because the need of the many outweigh the need of the few. So men by themselves steal aboard a train and become hoboes. And single women live with others in settlement houses or tenements, if not the YWCA.

Also there are a lot of kids moving about, because of their broken homes from poverty or the bad mental state in their homes. And they leave on a freight train too, and work any odd job they can get for as long as they can. In some cases, the young ones show their pathetic state-of-being, and beg for what they need to survive, or take to thieving. Also they travel in gangs and provide help for one another. Because of older adults who'd take advantage of them.

A large number of women have taken to the railroad as hoboes too, because they can no longer support themselves. The women cut their hair short and dress like men, to keep from being taken advantage of. She never wants to travel alone. Sometimes there's sexual activity for friendship, money, or food. Women on the road also work odd jobs as hoboes do. Usually you'll find them cleaning bathrooms in public places, and other kinds of cleaning up that needs to be done. Women are sleeping on park benches, and they're hoboes in hobo jungles. The rough living conditions are unbearable at times, like when she contracts lice, or fleas, the same as your pet.

Clarence is staying the night in the depot and so are a lot of other people. He found a place down on the floor to put himself until morning. A man there next to him is asleep and snoring loud. The dim light in the depot has it gloomy inside and shadows, with all of the people lying around motionless. The night lingers on and Clarence is sitting up—wide awake, because of the nap he took on the train coming to Tampa. On the outside of the depot, smoke from lighted cigars and cigarettes makes a gray fog in the air— intermixed with the dark in the night. Those inside can hear the talking from the ones smoking outside, but can't hear loud enough to follow what the words are saying.

Clarence is up and about bright and early the next day. He wants to know what time it is and how far off is the next passenger train. So he goes over to where the telegraph operator is to find out the details. "Say Mister, how long before the train gets here?" asks Clarence.

"It's half past seven o'clock now, and the next train is due in at nine fifteen. And it's supposed to be comin' without any other hitch-ups," answers the telegraph operator.

"That'll be good if there's no freight cars attached and we can keep straight ahead," says Clarence.

"Well now it's possible, that it'll go for some once it gets out there with you all aboard."

With that to consider, Clarence asks directions to a place for to eat. He is directed to a diner that he can very easily walk to from the depot. When he gets there, he sits on a bar stool at the bar.

"It's ok that you're in here because this ain't no whites only," says the cook to Clarence from the other side of the bar, where the grill for cooking is. He is a very tall and fat white man, about forty-five, with black-speckled gray hair.

"I didn't see no sign, so I came on in. And that's great too, 'cause I could eat a horse."

"You ain't from around here, are ya?"

"Nope. I came in on the train from Naples last night. And stayed in the depot, with all of the other people. I managed to get work-picking oranges so I can pay you for something to eat."

The cook gestures Clarence saying, "Ok" and then gets his breakfast. Which is biscuits and gravy. And he pours Clarence a cup of coffee.

"I got news for everyone that's waitin' on the passenger train due in this morning," says the telegraph operator who's at the depot. "It's held up for repairs. The cars can't get another engine hitch-up at this time," he continues. "They said over the wire it'll be the next two weeks at best," finishes the telegraph operator.

Clarence finishes eating and goes back to the depot. He gets the news as soon as he gets there.

"There's that fella. He come up from Naples and spent the night too," says a man in the depot referring to Clarence just after he walks in.

"That's right. I found me a diner near here, and got some breakfast."

"That sounds good, I wish I could have went with ya. But wait until you hear the news. The train ain't comin'. It's held up for repairs and they don't know what else," finishes the man in the depot at Clarence.

Clarence can only stand there in disgust for the moment. He decides to call Virginia again to make contact with his mother. He makes his way over to the telephone, but there's a long line of people ahead of him.

"You know that's really something the train ain't comin'," says Clarence to a woman standing in line just ahead of him.

"Yes, I know it. And like me, you'd better get you some other arrangements. Unless you can climb aboard a log roller that'll be coming in tonight," she continues. I suppose that's hows come you're in line for the telephone?" she finishes.

"No other arrangements yet. I thought I'd call my mother."

"Your mother, Don't you have a girl to come for ya— your wife maybe?"

"I did have a girl. She died of pneumonia this winter."

"Oh... well... now that's too bad. I'm sorry to hear that. Then it's good that you have your mother to rely on."

"It's not exactly that. You see, I'm on my way to Toledo, Ohio from Tidewater, Virginia. And since I been gone I ain't been able to talk to her." People standing in line are beginning to complain, that the ones talking on the phones already, are taking up too much time. And the complaining gets the line moving faster.

Clarence gets in touch with his mother this time and

talks to her, and her husband Nate as well. He explains his situation, and they tell him to be sure and call back when a train comes for him. After hanging up the telephone, Clarence goes outside to do some thinking. He is walking about, outside the depot — in thought about what next.

10

An Atlanta Georgia girl, whose name is Rhonda Smalls has decided to get aboard the next freight train leaving town as hoboes do. The color of her hair is black, and styled without the use of any aids for hair. It's the natural her African heritage is. She stands five feet, seven inches tall. And is a full figured woman. And at age thirty-five, her pearly whites are glossing through, and has her all so very confident. She's dressed in big mans mack clothes. She is wearing a man's brim on her head. At the present time there's not one steaming engine in sight to steal aboard. Her pockets are empty and the desperation for food has overtaken her. So she is going to a hobo jungle on the outer banks here in Atlanta, Georgia.

The streets are filled up with people moving about. Rhonda goes into the streets, walking down the sidewalks, turning corners. Finally she finds the hobo jungle, where people are camped out and as though piled on like garbage. There's a campfire burning in the jungle that has some sitting and some standing around it, that appear to be noble and just.

Rhonda Smalls dressed in her mans clothes goes over to greet the individuals.

"Hey...there, partners, my name's Rhonda Smalls. And I'm wondering what goes on around here. Maybe there's some extra food around, for a starving hobo like me?"

"There is, if 'n you was to help out with things hereabouts," answers a man who's sitting there.

"I'm willing to, so I can eat by."

"That's it, help with the cleaning up around here, and sometimes outside of here—in other places. Now that there's Addie Mae, She takes charge and puts ya to it."

"Yeah...that's me all right, and there's gathering up firewood to pitch on the fire," says Addie Mae.

"That's alright with me," says Rhonda Smalls.

"Good then you'll eat," finishes Addie Mae.

11

That night at the Tampa train station, a train comes steaming into the train yard with special made flat bed train cars full of logs stacked on, one on top of another. And there are giant sized iron chains roped around, to keep them all together.

"What about that freight there, what's it doing?" asks Clarence to a group of men, all of them standing around on the outside of the depot.

"That there is the cut timber, and it's on its way to Atlanta, Georgia from here," answers one of the men who's standing there.

"Yeah...that's right, it'll be gettin' come tomorrow morning," says one of the others.

Clarence has introduced himself to hopping trains at the start of his travels. And to hear them say the logs will be going north is like a melody. He has placed his bundle at his feet—the only soul possession to Clarence Taylor's concern at this time. He is standing there looking out at the train yard, and his imagination is running wild. He's dreaming of getting to the top of the cut timber and riding the train to Atlanta. He feels it'll be a better chance to take then to keep waiting there. Clarence is feeling the freedom of being out and about in his own way, and has set a mark and will enforce it.

The group of men has diminished, except for one. He sees Clarence standing there in thought.

"Sure... you're thinkin' about it. Just climbing aboard like I do. Thinking about it first is all a part of it."

Clarence turns to the voice that's just sounded off at him to see a not so very tall man standing there. He is in his forties the same as Clarence and dressed in rags, and wearing worn out boots on his feet.

"Oh...so you don't say," replies Clarence.

"That's right, you catch that one before it goes. You ever hop a train before?" he asks Clarence.

"Yeah...a freight train loaded with boxcars, coming from my home town in Virginia. But not those big logs on a flat bed."

"Ok, if 'n you want ta hear it, I'll fill ya in on it. Especially I can, that I'm hobo Ride 'em Jack cuttings. Its Ride 'em Jack because I can get aboard without benin' seen by the shacks, whereas no one else can. And I'm known up the southern coastline."

The night lingers on for Clarence Taylor and the hobo Ride 'em Jack. They have no real place to go and get with others to whom they really belong. So Clarence and his new acquaintance decide to bunk-out somewhere near the train station. They find an abandoned old broken down house.

"You and me can flop here for the night. I can see no one cares for this broken down old place," says ride 'em Jack.

"You're right about that, especially me," says Clarence.

"What's the matter, are you gettin' cold feet about it?"

"No, its this old house. It could be full of rats."

"Well, that's a chance you take. Rats, you know I've seen them on the railroad cars. Especially the food cars."

Clarence doesn't say anymore, he follows Ride 'em Jack into the house and spreads his bed roll out on the floor, the same as he did.

"What cha got back in your stash? Is it a bottle of whiskey? Maybe you found a whiskey maker, that boot-legs?" says Ride 'em Jack Cuttings.

"No, I aint been drinkin' but I got something to eat," says Clarence.

"Yeah...what cha got?"

"I got some biscuits kept back, but they're hard now. And there's some beef jerky, I manage to come by at the orange grove in Naples. And that's how's come I got these oranges, because I was picking them with the migrant workers down there. I had some apples too, but they're gone now. Do you want any of it?"

"Y...sure, I'll take some of that beef jerky. And two of them oranges."

Clarence eats some of his beef jerky as well, and one orange. They talk a bit more as they lie there, on their backs, looking up at the ceiling. Then the both of them slip off into deep sleep, and the both of them are snoring. Yet all is quiet and still at night.

12

Rhonda Smalls can hardly wait to get some of the baked bread that got to camp this morning. And she is standing in line for the cooked oats, as well. There's crying coming from behind her, its a woman crying out loud, with her face cuffed in her hands. And the small group of people about her is standing over the top of a dead body.

"He just now went this morning. As if 'n he couldn't hang on no more. I told 'em lets go to the dispensary, but he wouldn't go," says the very large black man, about his friend who had the tuberculosis.

"He was all I had and you people can help me get 'em buried," he continues.

Rhonda Smalls along with the others standing in line turns to see the tragedy. But she can't hear what the very large black man is saying.

One of the gents steps away from the small group of people, and goes over to where the food line is and sounds off.

"A man went this mornin,' jus' now. After hangin' on the best he could with that there tuberculosis. We all got ta pitch-in and help get 'em buried," he finishes. It's the friend of the very large black man who couldn't eat.

Rhonda Smalls, amazed at her new experience, gathers together with all of the people in the hobo jungle that she's become a part of to give her moral support.

Log roller with Clarence and Ride 'em Jack aboard

13

That morning's sun appears to be different in Florida. The Florida morning sun is very bright, and, already hot on one's face.

"That's good they got her steamin' already this mornin.' And the shacks aint paying any attention just yet at these logs—stacked on high," says Ride 'em Jack. After having slept the night through in an abandoned old house.

They 're quick to the train yard and have stolen aboard, to go to Georgia. "That's it, lay down flat so they can't see ya up there," says Ride 'em Jack. "Now come up here with me ta hang on, instead of back there on the tail end of the logs, and keep low so the shacks can't see ya," he continues. Without saying a word, Clarence down on all fours, crawls to the other end of the logs where Ride 'em Jack is waiting.

"Their ya are, that's good see...and when we get goin' grab hold and grip the chain tight. Until we 're good and straight on our way. Then you can get loose and more free of it. But you bare in mind, when the train takes a curve, you grip back tight," Ride 'em Jack explains.

From out of the depot comes the conductor, he gets aboard in the caboose. And the fireman is shoveling more coal for a hotter fire, so the train can get easily on its way.

"That's the last of them shacks ta get aboard. We'll be moving out now," says Ride 'em Jack. The engineer gets the train going on its way. And the powerful locomotive is switched from off one railroad track to another. And is now rolling on top of the ones that lead to Atlanta, Georgia.

At the top of its cargo the two hoboes have carefully placed themselves in the middle of a log. And they are holding on tight to the iron chains; that's got the logs held fast to the flat bed car cargo carrier. And riding high up, looking out at the country sites, Clarence Taylor takes in the view. It's like a gorgeous vista.

14

The Sea Board Air Line Railways in Tidewater Virginia rides the rails to Florida and comes back again and again.

"We're trying to strike up a deal with Florida, that gets us a contract with those people down there. Because we are so much back and forth with them. You see, that Flagler put all of those tracks down, that makes them good movement for conducting their business," says Mr. Foster.

"Oh yes, that's right, in Florida. And that's a good idea to try and get a contract ta do business with them." A member of the town council agrees with Mr. Foster's suggestion at the meeting they're having in the downtown office spaces, with its business consultants. Henry Flagler founded the Florida East Coast Railway company. After he obtained the Jacksonville

Saint Augustine and Halifax Railroad in the late 1800's. And Florida's biggest industries, tourism and agriculture is booming because of Flagler developing by way of the Model Land company. Flagler also built hotels and was a part of John D. Rockefeller and Samuel Andrews. All of them started standard oil. The Florida East Coast Railway also became the overseas railway attaching Key West to the mainland, and was completed in1912. And that's when Henry Flagler rode the first train into Key West, then died the next year.

"Florida can grow vegetables all year round," says Mr. Foster. "That can get us a good deal with them for our produce market up here in Virginia," he continues.

"Yes that's right, and theirs a lot of fruit that comes from them too," says a town council member. The seaboard here in Tidewater Virginia is already part of Flagler sea air line, that it goes to Jacksonville on a regular basis, common to its trains movements.

15

The log roller that has Clarence and Ride 'em Jack stolen aboard is stopping at a water tank just before the Macon County line.

"Now's a good time for me to carve my name on this water tank. Because I been missing it all of the other times that I've been coming up this way. And now the shacks are gonna get them a lunch 'n and won't be lookin' in this direction for awhile," says Ride 'em Jack Cuttings.

"You mean your gonna climb down and put your name on that water tank?" asks Clarence.

"Yeah sure...you put what your called. That's all a part of it."

"I never heard of that. And I had a chance to talk to someone before. He never told me nothin' about that."

"Oh yeah, just who did you talk to before?"

"He said he's Rails Trapeze Maxwell."

"Rails Trapezeee...I know him. You where with him?"

"Not exactly with 'em, he come from underneath, when the train stopped in South Carolina. We beat it to some trees and was hidin' behind 'em so the shacks couldn't see us. We talked then," says Clarence.

"Yeah... that would be him comin' from underneath, from off his board," says Ride 'em Jack.

"That's right, a board underneath he swings his ticket."

"He's a great hobo, but the last I heard, he's headed to Mississippi. Well, I guess not comin' from Virginia with you. He'd be in Florida now."

Ride 'em Jack tells Clarence to come with him because the shacks will be checking the load to make sure the chains are still held tight and has the logs fast to the flat bed train cars. Clarence climbs down as well and follows Ride 'em Jack to the water tank. Ride 'em Jack brings a pocket knife from his pocket and carves his moniker on the water tank.

"There Clarence, now you see."

"Yeah I see it."

"Well, I tell ya what. We're gonna have ta get ta callin' you something else too. Other than just Clarence Taylor, because that's your ordinary name, and that's gonna be too common. Now if I recall it, you say you started out in your town workin' at the depot when you was just a boy. Now aint that right Clarence?"

"Yes, that's right."

"Then it was Choo Choo trains ta you, when you first could see it. Choo choo trains, puff puffing down the railroad tracks, you thought then, I just bet cha," finishes Ride 'em Jack.

"Ha ha ha..." Clarence only laughs as he listens to Ride 'em Jack.

"That's it, Choo Choo Train Clarence Taylor. Now here, you carve it next to mine."

They both sit under a tree away from the train, where they can't be seen after that. And rummaged through their satchels for what they brought to eat.

In the dark, a big fire burning wooden boards and sticks piled on, is a glow in the night. And the hoboes in a hobo jungle here in Atlanta, Georgia have themselves sectioned off in their togetherness, with just whom it is to be together with.

"Mommy are we gonna eat some more tonight?"

"I told you that'll be it until tomorrow morning Samuel, when we was getting supper. Then their's oatmeal for breakfast."

"Yeah, but I couldn't hardly eat supper mommy. Because it was beans again."

"Still, you have to wait until tomorrow morning."

Rhonda Smalls is over by the campfire, where she manages to intermix with some others. She too wants some other food to eat. Because Rhonda never required the taste for navy beans or any beans of any kind. But it's a free offering from the gathering of the jungle, so she doesn't complain. Her expression is that of thanksgiving instead. Therefore the uncomfortable situation is a matter for new direction, because there she will not stay.

"I see you all are making yourselves at home here the best you can," says Rhonda Smalls.

"Yeah that's right, its not home, but we have this ideal for now," a lady replies back to Rhonda who's sitting there.

"I have an idea that I'm gonna go north to Ohio, where my aunt lives. She's my mother's sister. And she has her husband Chester, and my two cousins, Philip and Phyllis, they're twins and only three years younger then me," says Rhonda.

"Where in Ohio is that?" a man asks.

"In Toledo," answers Rhonda.

"I see... I wished I had somewheres ta go," the man again.

All of a sudden they become silent as they sit there, outdoors in the night.

When Choo Choo Train Clarence Taylor and Ride 'em Jack get to Atlanta Georgia, they want to find another empty house to fall a sleep in. The train ride was long and stressful from hanging on.

"I need me another good night sleep," says Choo Choo Train.

"Yeah... if 'n we can find somewheres ta get into," says

ride 'em Jack. They've walked away from the depot. And the dark at this time of night has it very black outside. There are some others moving about, and they're desperate for money. Also the not so good environment is spooky with its run down buildings and trashed out houses.

"Maybe there's a vacant place in those houses over there we can get into," says Choo Choo Train.

"Well... maybe there is. But you wait a minute. There's a jungle that got started just on the outside of town. Usually I go there, and there's running water too. So you can clean up. And sometimes you can get work," says ride 'em Jack.

The dwellings got called hobo jungles because the hoboes pitched themselves in the weeds and grassy fields. And they built shelters out of all kinds of stuff they found thereabouts.

"That's fine by me if you want to go there."

"Yep, that I do. But it's best ta get there in the daytime. Exceptin' they'll remember me from before, and you'll be ok that your with me."

With Ride 'em Jack Cuttings in the lead, he and Choo Choo Train Clarence Taylor set out for the hobo jungle. Some klankering trucks and cars comes roaring past, and they stick their thumbs out to hitch a ride, but no one stops in the dark.

"Well, here we are Choo Choo Train, you see it out there?"

"Yes I see it, that's some camp fire burning. And look at all of the people."

Some hobo jungles go for miles, and this one's a similitude.

"Sure... hopefully we can get some Mulligan stew. That's whatever food scrounged up and put in the pot ta eat," explains Ride 'em Jack.

"And I'll eat it," says Choo Choo Train. They both go into the jungle and appear as two shadows cast on everybody sitting near the fire. Almost everyone sees the two individuals, and wish to hear any spreading of the news they have to tell. The both of them are the same itinerants that's to the hobo camp.

"Who might cha be that wanders in ta camp this time of the night," asks one of the hoboes sitting there.

"Y... its me, Ride 'em Jack Cuttings."

"Oh, you don't say. Its Ride 'em Jack. I can see ya now by the light of the fire," another one chimes in.

"You do remember me from before?"

"Yeah I do, he's been comin' and going."

"That's right about me. And this here is Choo Choo Train Clarence Taylor, he just now is."

"Oh, so you don't say..."

"Well, come some closer sosss...'n we can get a look at ya, Choo Choo Train." There's a lot of them speaking up now, and Ride 'em Jack is recognized by some others.

"You best speak up on your own now," says Ride 'em Jack.

"We just came up from Florida on a big log roller," says Choo Choo Train.

"That's right, cut timber out of Florida for the saw mills up here," says Ride 'em Jack.

"But at first I hopped on a boxcar coming out of Tidewater Virginia, because that's where I'm from. It was supposed to be going north to Ohio. Except it switch tracks and come south. I'm still trying to get north," finishes Choo Choo Train Clarence Taylor.

"We was wantin' ta get some Mulligan stew, if 'n there's any," says Ride 'em Jack.

"Not no Mulligan, it's navy beans. We manage to flavor it though, with some Joe meat and salt and pepper. You go ahead to what's left, down in the pot."

There aren't any dishes to eat with, so they have to make up a difference with whatever they can.

"Here's you a plate," says Ride 'em Jack.

"This is a tomato can," says Choo Choo Train.

"That's right and its flattened out, see...next we'll go over there and break off a small branch. That'll be the spoon and fork."

They can put one full ladle down on the flat tomato can. And then they sit on the ground with the other hoboes. Ride 'em Jack seats himself with the ones he knows.

"Ya know what Ride 'em. You should have stayed in Florida and cut timber. Because they're gonna be at that down there, and back 'n forth 'n it."

"I know it, I did do some. I needed to get away from it

after awhile. Besides, I know of some other goings on due west of here."

"Yeah...so ya don't say."

"That's right, something other. I'll tell ya but cha gotta keep quiet."

"Ok, I'm quiet."

"Its mining for gold."

"Mining for gold you say?"

"Ssshh... hold your voice down, I said. Yep, they're gettin' that out there—panning for it in the creeks and rivers. That's in the Oklahomie and up to the Montanans and Missouri, around by ole saint Louie, that is."

Choo Choo Train is sitting a little ways off from the lot of them. And he's able to eat the navy beans that's upon the flattened out tomato can, by using the small branch for a utensil. A hobo sitting near the fire moves over to where Choo Choo Train is and sits with him.

"Those beans aint bad hu?" the hobo says to Choo Choo Train.

"I'll eat 'em," he replies.

"They got fixed up earlier this evening so their good ta eat if you're hungry enough. But that's all its been around here is beans."

"Ride 'em Jack was saying something about Mulligan stew."

"I aint seen none, but I only been here for a couple of days. There'll be oatmeal in the morning."

The Journey

"In the morning is just fine by me, then I gotta get movin' on."

"I heard you saying that you'll be headin' to Ohio."

"That's right. That's right, Toledo to be exact."

"I'd like to travel to Ohio with ya."

"You got any money?"

"Are you kiddin,' you don't have it either, bein's that your a hobo in a hobo jungle."

"I did have something, I got me a ticket for the passenger train in Naples, Florida. And we had a layover in Tampa. Then it's not coming. That's all I know, is it needed fix 'n, then it's not coming. So I hopped on board the log roller. That's when I ran into Ride 'em Jack Cuttings."

"I see, so you know what it is to hop a train?"

"That's right, pretty much. I first did in Virginia like I said."

"That's swell. You see, I'm wantin' to go to Toledo Ohio, because I got some people up there. So when ya goin,' can I go too?"

Choo Choo Train is uneasy about the request coming from the hobo who approached him. He doesn't say anything for a few moments, but can't help to stare as he eats.

"How old are you?" he asks.

"I'm old enough, lots old enough."

"Its to dark to see."

"Well, that's because it's so blackout around here, this time at night. And we're away from the fire."

"Yeah...but the sound of you too. Sounds to me like a kid."

"Lets you and me talk again in the morning. Its time I turn in right now for the ones I bunk with. Now you'll still be here come morning?"

"Yes, it looks like I'll be sleeping out here by the fire." The hobo that had approached Choo Choo Train disembark, and Choo Choo Train along with Ride 'em Jack, dip the ladle down into the giant pot once more. And then they sit together against the big lengthy log.

"You and me will be bedding down here tonight," says Ride 'em Jack.

"Yep, it looks that way to me," says Choo Choo Train.

"Did you hear me when I said I'll be pulling out tomorrow?" says Ride 'em Jack.

"No, you were talkin' too quiet. And someone came over to me and got my attention," says Choo Choo Train.

"Well, anyways I'll be headin' West, come morning. You should be alright around here now, for as long as you still need ta be here," says Ride 'em Jack.

"Ok, and that'll be good bye, because I'm still headed north," finishes Choo Choo Train.

"Yeah...now let's let that do it. I need to get rolling over and go to sleep. But there's just one more thing. You be sure and sack out yourself, and don't be up stirring about. Because something can wind up missing come morning and you could get the blame for Jackrolling. Jackrolling means you was thievin.' And here you get stoned or beaten for it. And you make for certain that you finish your plate too. Because they don't like wasting food either," finishes Ride 'em Jack Cuttings.

"I know what cha mean about thievin.' The deputy in my town shot two hoboes cought thievin.' The first one was a long time ago, I was a little boy then. And the other one just last year in the fall. And it was an amazing thing to me too, about him. Because we had just been fishing down at the river," says Choo Choo Train.

"Oh no, now you see those weren't no hoboes. Them's was tramps or yeags."

"It looked like hoboes, as we are now, and what's around here."

"It intermixes, tramps and yeags are here in the jungle the same— now that's right. Those ones would rather beg for it or steal it, rather than work. Another name for yeags is Johnsons. They live in Johnson families, too. That's them to themselves sharing food and telling their stories. But you see now, a hobo is hard working and honorable," explains Ride 'em Jack.

Some of the other hoboes spend the night outdoors by the campfire as well. But the most of them is in their little shack built there in the weeds from scrap. Choo Choo Train pitches more wood on the fire and lays down for the final time that night. There is no sounds of music or any people talking.

One can only hear the crackling of the fire and the howling of the wind.

16

And the night passing happens very peacefully for the small Virginian town here in Tidewater. The morning has come and patriotism zealously is about the individual. To support one's own country and then it's off into the fatherland.

"Us democrats are gonna get Franklin Delano Roosevelt elected come this here election."

"That's right, there's been to much desperation for us by now. And I believe Roosevelt is on the right track, with progress for the labor force of America."

"Yes, the economic collapse has done us in bad enough. That we must get relief immediately."

Franklin Delano Roosevelt is campaigning the most confident and the best energy. To get something exact for immediate relief and reform measures. The patriotic people here in Tidewater Virginia, have gathered together and discuss the matter.

"That's it Barbo, move it over just a little more," says Haddy. She and Barbo Brown are centering an inspirational picture of praying hands up on the wall in the Annex at their church, where there is the soup kitchen.

"Ok, I'll mark this spot and put a nail there, then hang the picture up on it," says Barbo Brown.

The both of them are elderly and help build the church when it first came about. Sally and her husband Nate are at home and still sitting at the breakfast table. She cooked some bacon and scrambled eggs and stir-fried some cut potatoes. Nate is dressed in his clothes, Sally though is still in her slumber. They agree that unemployment is a very big reason for the depression. Its got business at a big stand still as far as their fullest potential. And with so many people without work, cities have gradually exhausted their strength. Sally's neighbor Gretchen from across the street is knocking at the door. Sally arises from the breakfast table and buttons up her robe, as she goes for the door.

"Good morning Gretchen, come in."

"I thought I'd come over and sit with you for awhile this morning."

"That's good because Nate is about to leave. He's got work at the saw mill these next few days, and I can use some company."

Nate only sits smiling at the two ladies as they come

into the kitchen. He finishes eating and heads for the door.

"No one's called for you Sally, but I wonder about Clarence. If he's made it to Toledo, Ohio by now or not."

"It could be that he did, we'll just have to wait for him to call again. And by the way, Gretchen, we're able to get a phone installed with the money Nate's getting from out at the sawmill this time. And then we can communicate better around here."

"It sounds like you and Nate've been making plans."

"We try to be prepared for whatever happens."

Sally begins cleaning the kitchen as she and Gretchen talk a bit more. Afterwards Sally takes a bath and gets dressed for the day. She walks to the nearby bus stop so she can get to Jane Somer's hat shop, and the bus comes on schedule. Sally enters into the hat shop where Jane is talking with Mary.

"Hi Sally, come on in and sit down," says Jane.

"Its good to see ya this afternoon, it's been a few days and we're gettin' to wonder about ya," says Mary.

"I been home, that's all. I decided to get out today and come see what you all been up to," replies Sally.

17

And after the morning passes by, Rhonda Smalls makes her way back to where the fire burned in the night. Other hoboes are already there, as though it's a meeting place within the domains of the hobo jungle.

"Fifteen got out ta work this morning," says one of the hoboes standing there.

"Fifteen ain't very many. We need fifty or even a hundred of us everyday," replies one of the others.

"Did anyone hear what they're doing and how much work it is?"

"It's doing odd jobs around town, for three days is what I know."

Typically, the hoboes are standing around talking work and there's no work. And what their next meal is going to be.

"I saw you eat the oats this morning like I did. That'll tide you over until there's something else."

"Yeah...that's right."

"You're still here huh?"

"Yep, but there's a train pulling out tonight. I'll be leaving then."

"Do you remember me from last night? I ask to go with ya."

"Oh yeah, that's you. And you're a girl. I can't tell it in the dark, and the clothes you're wearing threw me too. You got a name?"

"Yes, it's Rhonda. I'm Rhonda Smalls. And you're Choo Choo Train Clarence Taylor. I heard that Ride 'em Jack say it when he announced it."

"He went out this morning in a automobile with a fella going west. Their gonna pan for gold. Its gold prospecting is what he said."

Rhonda finds Choo Choo Train in the same place as before. The hobo jungle is full of people this time of the day. And there are all races of people in its domains. All of them are poor people, but manage to clean up by establishing the encampment near running water. And the hoboes share in everything, especially the food as well as other supplies. They wash there clothes in big pots of boiling water, one item at a time. And make sure the wash kills any unwanted parasites that may be contained in them.

Choo Choo Train plans to hop a train after it leaves the

Union Station, bound for Chattanooga Tennessee, and Lexington Kentucky. He may have to work again with the migrant workers.

"You ever hop a train before?" he asks Rhonda Smalls.

"No, but I think I can."

"You're gonna have to, tonight if you plan to tag along with me."

"That's how I thought you'd get it on. I can manage it."

"Ok, we'll see. There's gonna be a cargo train coming in tonight loaded down with freight, and it's headed north of here. I got that first rate this morning from one of the hoboes that's here. You and me are gonna get on that one, you understand?"

"Yes."

"I tell ya what else, since you'll be traveling with me."

"What?"

"There may be a time when we'll have to work with the migrant workers. Just like we was one."

"That suits me just fine, too. Anything beats mopin' around here, down and out as it is." Rhonda seems confident enough to Choo Choo Train that he is relaxed, sitting there talking it out with her.

And so is the city of Atlanta Georgia depleted of its resources. Pawnshops are always filled up with people, pawning what little they still have of value. And what savings there is ran out, those vehicles necessary for transport to the individual got repossessed, and the foreclosure of homes.

Desperate families had to get relief, but there are so many that the city system cut back payment to a very big extent. More people are in bread lines and soup kitchens now, who thought they'd never be. And the hoboes still journey—there'll be something better in the next town.

At dusk, Choo Choo Train Clarence Taylor and Rhonda Smalls find themselves walking alongside of the road that leads to town. On the road Clarence Taylor is becoming more and more the new role in life he's chosen to take on. It's another kind of talking and new customs on the road being one of the itinerant workers, rather than to have stayed in his small Virginian town. The both of them are up in spirits about their togetherness. Because they realize life on the road is going to be dangerous. There's hunger, disease and loneliness. However, its the possibility of opportunities that gets them on their way.

"Come on, Choo Choo Train, stick your thumb out like me."

"That ain't gonna do no good, because they won't stop."

"Yes, they're gonna. Ain't cha ever hitched a ride before?"

"Me and Ride 'em Jack tried it and they wouldn't stop. It was like now too. Only headed the way we just come. And it was at night, close to the time it is now, except it was dark out."

"Oh yeah! Well, just you look now! He's stoppin' lets go catch 'em!"

A man-driving pass in his pick-up truck yields Rhonda's thumbing. "Hello Mister, him and me's together, do you want us to hop in the back?"

"You two can ride up in the front with me."

"Alright, then. Come on, Choo Choo Train, he said to ride up front."

"That's right, get in and lets go. Besides, you can't get back there, because I have all of my stuff in the back."

Rhonda is sitting in the middle of the both of them. The driver of the truck gets back up on the road from off the side. "I can see you two are headed in to town the same as me," says the man who has the pick up truck.

"Yeah, that's right," answers Rhonda.

"I'm goin' for the Sally that's in the downtown, because I can't pay for my place out there no more. You see, I was living in the country their abouts. I was apart of the wheat harvesting, before a drought took us out. And I can't recover for the way it is now. So I lost it all, is how's come I'm coming pass."

"You're gonna go to the Sally?" asks Choo Choo Train.

"Yeah... that's the Salvation Army," answers Rhonda.

"That's right, there may be some doings there in town. That's the best I can figure it," says the driver.

"How's about everybody else, where's your family?" asks Rhonda.

"I never took ta gettin' married. Just only had myself.

As for the rest of it, my brother and two sisters, that's all I got me, are scattered about here in Georgia," he finishes.

"I see, we'll be gettin' out thereabouts," says Rhonda."

Once they get there, Rhonda Smalls and Choo Choo Train Clarence Taylor head out past the Union Station, where they plan to hop aboard the train. There are a lot of hoboes at the Sally, and some yeags and bums. Unemployment reaches black African Americans beyond all of the other persons nationally. And the undesirable jobs most blacks are working now is good to have, because of the unemployment rate for all people. White people are saying they want Negroes to work jobs as being domestic servants. There are some white people in Atlanta with a slogan saying, "No jobs for niggers until every white man has a job."

And here in 1932 the number of lynchings in America has increased.

"Well here we are Choo Choo Train, this be the place."

"Yeah...this is perfect."

"When the train comes I guess we'll take out running and catch-up to it."

"That's right, and when we get to it you be sure and just get on board, Rhonda. When you grab hold you pull your legs up and hold tight, and get ta climbin,' and don't you slip off. You keep a grip."

He leaves it to Rhonda's imagination as to what it could be like if she slips off. Rhonda just only stares at him and listens. But she is full of excitement, and eager to hop a train bound for where her aunt lives in Toledo, Ohio.

Now it is completely dark outside in the night. The shacks have walked the tracks to look the train over a final time before leaving, and have found nothing. After all are aboard, and releasing the breaks, the train gets moving out. Choo Choo Train and Rhonda Smalls are both slumped down in the shadows, behind trees and brush near the train tracks where it'll be coming past. It's as though all of a sudden that it's coming past, even though its been sometime waiting. They come running as fast as they can from where they were waiting. And alongside of an open boxcar they're able to keep up. First, Choo Choo Train throws his satchel into the open boxcar and places both hands firmly down on it and heaves up and tosses himself inside.

"Come on, run faster and get closer!" he shouts at Rhonda as she's trying to catch the train too.

"I'm running as fast as I can!" Choo Choo Train leans out with his hand extended, reaching for Rhonda. She moves in closer and throws her satchel in, and has a hand reaching as well.

"Ok, I got ya. Jump up and in before they see us." All in one motion just when their hands grip together, she leaps to Choo Choo Train and he pulls her in.

And now the both of them have fallen on the floor of the boxcar, and gain control of themselves, then sit up— looking out at the outdoors. The dark is lit by the moon enough to see trees and buildings as well as some houses, in a distance. "Choo Choo Train, look there! Can you see 'em?"

He moves closer to the opening of the boxcar where she is and can see another hobo coming for the train as they just did. But the train is going faster now and he can't keep steady along the side. Still, he leaps for a ladder that's to a boxcar and gets a hold of it, barely hanging on.

"He got it but he can't hardly hold on!" shouts Rhonda.

"I see 'em!" Choo Choo Train chiming in.

"Oh no, he can't get his feet up!" Rhonda again.

"He's not gonna make it because we're goin' too fast!" shouts Choo Choo Train. Seeing out of the boxcar, they both can see the hobo is barely hanging on to the ladder. His legs and the boots on his feet are dangling and swaying—swinging. The time passing now is like a long time passing. But its only been a few moments. And the hobo hasn't the strength to keep hanging on and lets go. He falls and the powerful moving locomotive sucks him underneath. And just when he's hitting, the hobo screams out very horrible knowing it's the death of him, and Rhonda screams out too. She and Choo Choo Train can't help but embrace each other. And they are holding on tight because they manage to get aboard, instead of falling.

"Try not to look at it anymore, Rhonda."

"I aint lookin.' "

"Ok, but still you wait until we get further down the tracks before you go ta lookin' out."

She nods her head as they separate, then they sit side by side and far enough back in the boxcar to only see in front of them.

91

"I'll be sure and catch a train when it's going slow enough," says Rhonda.

"That's right, it's going too fast now," says Choo Choo Train.

Still, there are some who remain in Atlanta and Virginia. The both of them stolen aboard at this time have feelings of being the outcast. And even though they have direction, the big guarantee that things are going to work out is besides them. If only they really knew.

Printed in the United States
by Baker & Taylor Publisher Services